Dear Parent:
Your child's love of reading s...

D0315147

Every child learns to read in a different way and at his or her own speed. Some go back and forth between reading levels and read favorite books again and again. Others read through each level in order. You can help your young reader improve and become more confident by encouraging his or her own interests and abilities. From books your child reads with you to the first books he or she reads alone, there are I Can Read Books for every stage of reading:

SHARED READING
Basic language, word repetition, and whimsical illustrations, ideal for sharing with your emergent reader

BEGINNING READING
Short sentences, familiar words, and simple concepts for children eager to read on their own

READING WITH HELP
Engaging stories, longer sentences, and language play for developing readers

READING ALONE
Complex plots, challenging vocabulary, and high-interest topics for the independent reader

ADVANCED READING
Short paragraphs, chapters, and exciting themes for the perfect bridge to chapter books

I Can Read Books have introduced children to the joy of reading since 1957. Featuring award-winning authors and illustrators and a fabulous cast of beloved characters, I Can Read Books set the standard for beginning readers.

A lifetime of discovery begins with the magical words "I Can Read!"

Visit www.icanread.com for information
on enriching your child's reading experience.

I Can Read!

BEGINNING
1
READING

Pinkalicious®

The Princess of Pink
Slumber Party

For Jennifer and Sydney
—V.K.

The author gratefully acknowledges
the artistic and editorial contributions
of Jared Osterhold and Natalie Engel.

I Can Read Book® is a trademark of HarperCollins Publishers.

Pinkalicious: The Princess of Pink Slumber Party
Copyright © 2012 by Victoria Kann

PINKALICIOUS and all related logos and characters are trademarks of Victoria Kann. Used with permission.

Based on the HarperCollins book Pinkalicious written by
Victoria Kann and Elizabeth Kann, illustrated by Victoria Kann
All rights reserved. Manufactured in China.
No part of this book may be used or reproduced in any manner whatsoever without
written permission except in the case of brief quotations embodied in critical articles and reviews.
For information address HarperCollins Children's Books, a division of HarperCollins Publishers,
195 Broadway, New York, NY 10007.
www.icanread.com

Library of Congress catalog card number: 2011940620

ISBN 978-0-06-198963-6 (trade bdg.) — ISBN 978-0-06-198962-9 (pbk.)

18 19 20 SCP 10 9 8 7 6
❖
First Edition

I Can Read!

BEGINNING 1 READING

Pinkalicious®

The Princess of Pink Slumber Party

by Victoria Kann

HARPER
An Imprint of HarperCollinsPublishers

I was having a slumber party.

It was not any old slumber party.

It was a Princess of Pink party!

My whole family got ready.
Mommy and Daddy dressed up
like a queen and a king.

"I'm the royal prince," said Peter.

He grabbed a crown out of my hand.

"You're more like a royal joker,"
I told him.

DING DONG!

"The princesses are here!" I said.

I twirled my way to the door

and let my royal friends in.

"Welcome," I said with a curtsy.

"Enter the castle, fair maidens!"

"How grand!" Molly said.

"I'm ready for the ball!" Rose said.

"Hello, Princess Alison," I said.

"Hi," Alison said quietly.

She held her bear tightly.

"Let's play musical thrones!"

I started the music

and we danced around the chairs.

I didn't even mind being

the last one left without a throne.

12

"Yay! I won!" said Molly.

"Your prize, Your Majesty," I said.

I handed Molly a pinkatastic wand.

"It's time to make tiaras!" I said.

"Ohhhh," Rose said.

"Look at the dazzling jewels!"

"My tiara is going to twinkle

like a star," said Molly.

"Look at me," I said.

I put my tiara proudly on my head.

"I have the sparkliest tiara

in all the land!"

"Dinner is served!" said Mommy.

"We made a royal feast," said Daddy.

"Princess-and-the-Split-Pea Soup,

Chicken Nuggets à la King,

and Castle Cupcakes for dessert!"

Peter said, "If I was ruler,

we'd always eat dessert first!"

"Yum," I said.

"That would be a very sweet kingdom!"

After dinner Peter climbed

to the top of a pile of pillows

and yelled, "I'm king of the castle!"

"It's princess of the castle
around here," I said.

"Princesses rule!" Molly said.

Suddenly I heard a sniffle.

It came from Alison.

"What's wrong?" I asked her.

"I'm scared to sleep over,"

she whispered in my ear.

I gave Alison a hug.

"Sleeping away from home

can be kind of scary," I said.

"What would a real princess do
to make Alison feel better?" I asked.

"Protect her from villains!" Rose said.

"A princess faces her perils
with strength," Molly said.

Alison still looked scared.

"I know!" I said.

"A real princess would have
a dragon to protect her!"

"Close your eyes," I said.

"Unlock the magic kingdom!

What do you see?"

"Nothing," said Alison.

24

"Listen!" I said.

"Do you hear the dragon
walking in the enchanted forest?"

"That's your dad walking down the hall,"
Rose said.

"Breathe!" I said.

"Do you smell the odor
of dragon breath in the air?"

"Oh, excuse me," Molly said.

"I just burped!"

"Wait!" I said.

"Don't you hear the loud beating
of the dragon's heart?"

"That is my heart," said Rose.

"I've never seen a dragon before!"

"Now open your eyes," I said.

"The dragon is here!

It is pink and it is breathing fire.

Look how spiky its tail is!"

"I see the dragon!" Alison said.

"It is sparkling in the moonlight."

The dragon smiled.

"She will protect us," I said.

"What do you think

the dragon's name is?" Rose asked.

Alison yawned.

"Can I tell you in the morning?

I'm so sleepy," Alison said.

"Goodnight, Princesses of Pink,"

I said.

"Goodnight, dragon," we all said.

Outside, the dragon winked.